5 Minute Farm Tales

LITTLE TIGER PRESS
London

Contents

Dilly Duckling

Claire Freedman   Jane Chapman

One sunshiny day, the Ducks set off for a family waddle. Little Dilly was last in the line.

"Peekaboo!" Dilly said to the fish.
"Hello!" she called to the bugs
and dragonflies.

"Keep up, Dilly!" Mummy
Duck called. But Dilly was busy
watching a big blue butterfly.

She waddled after it when suddenly,
PUFF! a gust of wind blew out one
of her downy feathers!
  "Oh no!" gasped Dilly. "My feather!
It's flying away!"

Dilly raced after the big fluffy feather.

"Stop that feather!" she quacked loudly.

Wheeee!

The wind blew Dilly's downy feather this way
and that way . . . up in the air . . . and down again.

Round and round in circles ran Dilly dizzily, trying to catch it.

"Come back!" she called to her feather. But it floated further and further away.

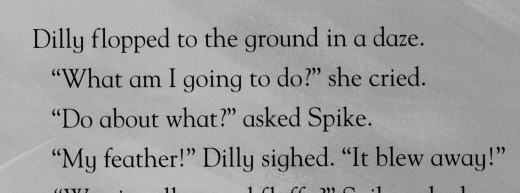

Dilly flopped to the ground in a daze.

"What am I going to do?" she cried.

"Do about what?" asked Spike.

"My feather!" Dilly sighed. "It blew away!"

"Was it yellow and fluffy?" Spike asked.

"Yes!" cried Dilly excitedly.

"It drifted down the hill!" Spike said.

"I'll get it!"

15

Spike curled himself into a tight ball.
He rolled downhill, spinning faster and faster.
    "I'll try to spear your feather on my spikes!"
he shouted as he whizzed by.

"Wheeeeee!" Spike cried.
"Hooray!" quacked Dilly excitedly.

Bump! Spike landed in a hedge.
Puff! Up flew Dilly's feather again!
Slowly, it drifted down, down, down,
until it landed in a field.

Dilly and Spike pitter-pattered after it.

"It's caught on a corn stalk!" squeaked Nibble. "I'll get it for you!"

"Careful!" whispered Dilly.
"It's a very important feather!"

Nibble held her breath as she crept through the tall grass. Slowly she climbed the corn stalk and gently stretched out her paw . . .

"Atchoo!" sneezed Nibble as the
feather tickled her twitchy nose!
Wheeee! Off Dilly's feather flew.

The wind blew Dilly's feather up, up in the sky and far, far away.

"Sorry, Dilly!" Nibble called. "It's gone!"

"OH NO!" quacked Dilly, and she burst into tears.

"Oh, poor Dilly," said Spike.
"Don't cry!"
Nibble and Spike gave little
Dilly a 'cheer up' hug.

"I'll never see my fluffy feather again,"
Dilly sighed sadly. "I'm going home to tell
my mummy."

Dilly waved her friends goodbye. "Thank
you for trying to help me," she called.

"Mummy!" Dilly quacked. "One of my big
fluffy feathers has fallen out! It's lost forever!"

"Silly Dilly!" Mummy Duck said, giving
Dilly a big cuddle. "ALL your downy feathers
will fall out. Then you'll grow new grown-up
feathers – just like mine!"

"Really?" quacked Dilly in surprise.
"So I'll look just like you!"

Dilly and Mummy Duck joined the
ducklings splashing in the river.

"Look!" Dilly cried. "There's my feather!"

"So it is!" said Mummy Duck.

"I don't need it any more, do I?" Dilly
giggled. "I'll grow another one!"

And quacking happily, she
dilly-dallied off to play!

Don't Be So Nosy, Posy!

Nicola Grant

Tim Warnes

Posy the piglet didn't mean to be nosy. She was just terribly interested in knowing things.

"Who wakes *you* up each morning?" she asked Ronny Rooster.

"Does it hurt to lay an egg?" she said to Hetty Hen.

"Questions, questions!"
the animals sighed. "Don't be
so nosy, Posy!"

But Posy wanted to learn
things. Even if it did sometimes
land her in trouble!

One morning, Posy was playing
'don't tread on the daisies' with
Cowslip Cow. As they skipped under
an oak tree they heard a strange noise.
"I wonder what that is?" said Posy,
peering inside a hollow in the oak to look.
"Oooh! Don't do that, Posy!"
cried Cowslip, but it was too late . . .

ZZZZZZZZZZZZZZZZZZZZZZZZ!

Posy raced off quickly, chased
by some very cross bees!
  "Oh Posy, you do look funny!"
Cowslip laughed. "You've got
honey all over your nosy nose!"

The next day, Posy was playing in the farmyard when she spotted the farmer's tractor nearby.

"I wonder what *this* does?" she said, pressing a big red button.

BEEEEEEP! blasted the horn. Posy tumbled out in a heap!

"Who's playing with my tractor?" yelled
the farmer, running up.
"It's Nosy Posy!" clucked Hetty Hen crossly.
"And she's woken me from my nap!"
"Sorry!" Posy squealed. "I'll try to play more quietly!"
But Posy couldn't stay quiet for long!

43

"Do you feel chilly without your warm woolly fleece?" she asked Sally Sheep on shearing day. "Tell me, do you keep noses in your nose-bag?" she laughed at Harry Horse.

"How silly!" mumbled Harry. "One day you'll learn not to be so nosy, Posy!"

But Posy didn't think so!

Then, one sunny day, Posy and Dilly and
Dally Duck were playing piggybacks.
"Ooooooooooh!" came a strange noise from
somewhere across the field.

"What was that?" Posy said excitedly. "Let's find out!"

"Don't be nosy, Posy!" quacked Dilly and Dally.

"Whatever it is, it sounds scary!"

"Scaredy ducks!" Posy laughed back. "Come on!"

They crept closer . . . and closer . . . until they saw . . .

. . . Cowslip Cow with her head stuck in a fence!

"Oh, Posy," Cowslip cried. "I squeezed through here to reach some tasty clover, and now I'm trapped. Please help me!"

Posy and the ducks pulled and pushed but Cowslip was stuck fast!

"I'll never get out!" howled Cowslip. "My head will drop off! Help me, Posy!"

OOOOOOO!

"The farmer will rescue you!" said Posy.
So they all cried out at the tops of their
voices: "HELP! HELP! HELP!"

But the farmer was too far away to hear.

"I'm stuck here forever!" And a big tear
fell from Cowslip's eye with a plop!

Then, out of the corner of her eye, Posy
spotted something that was sure to bring the
farmer running . . .

The tractor!

52

Posy pressed the tractor's horn.

BEEEEEEEEEEEEEEEP!

Up the field raced the farmer!
And behind him came all the other
animals, clucking and squawking,
neighing and bleating, to see what
was happening.

"Oh dear me!" cried the farmer.
"Right, everyone. You all push, and
Harry and I will pull. After three.

One . . .

TWO . . .

THREE!"

"Heave!" gasped the animals.

"Squeeze!" shouted the farmer.

"Ooooh!" gulped Cowslip.

Suddenly there was a very

loud OOMPH!

Everybody cheered. Cowslip was free!
"Hoorah for Nosy Posy!" she mooed
happily. "If it wasn't for her, I could have
been stuck there forever!"

"It was nothing!" said Posy proudly.

"We'll never complain about your
questions again!" the animals told
Posy. "In fact, you can ask us
anything you want!"

"OK! What's this for, Dilly?" Posy
asked, looking at a large blue
hosepipe lying nearby.

"And what happens
when you turn
this big handle?"

You're Too Small!

Shen Roddie

Steve Lavis

Pip woke up all warm and
tingly as a dot of sunshine
touched his nose.

He peered out of the
window.
   "Everyone's busy!"
he piped. "I'll run down
and help."

Pig was pushing a barrow
of marrows.

"I'll help you," said Pip.

"Better not," said Pig. "You're
too small. You'd get squashed."

Nearby, Goat was stacking hay.

"Can I help?" asked Pip.

"No thank you," said Goat.

"You're too small. You'd get lost."

Pip ran off and
found Cow. She was
painting a wall.

"I can help!" said Pip.

"I don't think so," said Cow. "You're too small. You'd never reach the top."

"Well," thought Pip, "if I'm too small to help, I'll just have to go and play!"

He skipped off into the fields where he met Rabbit, flying a kite.

"Can I have a go?" asked Pip.

"No!" said Rabbit. "You're too small. You'd get blown away!"

Pip looked at himself.
He looked at his big paws,
his round belly and
his long tail.
   "I don't look small to me!"
he said. "I look just right!"
Then he asked, "Goose,
do you think I'm the right
size to sit on your eggs?
After all, you don't look
very big yourself!"

Goose took a deep breath.
Then she stood up . . . taller . . .
and taller . . .

   "Pip," she said, peering
down at him. "I would love
you to sit on my eggs but
you wouldn't cover them at
all. You are just too small!"

"Oh dear," said Pip. "I think I'll go back
to bed and start again tomorrow. Perhaps
I'll have grown some more by then."
   Pip walked slowly back to the barn.
But when he got to
the door . . .

. . . there was a big hubbub! All his friends were there, banging on the door.

"Pig came to tell us dinner was ready and the door slammed behind him. We're all locked out!" cried Rabbit.

"And we're starving!" said Goose.

"I can help," said Pip. And he disappeared . . .

. . . through a crack in the wall.

"I'm just small enough!"
he called from inside.

"Hurray for Pip! Hurray!
Hurray! Hurray!" everyone
cheered.

But since dinner
was all ready . . .

. . . Pip hopped on to the table.
"There's another thing I'm not
too small for . . ." he smiled, as
he helped himself to the biggest,
plumpest puffed-up pie!

Then he hopped off the table,
unlocked the door . . . and let
his hungry friends in.
   "Thank you, Pip!" they shouted.
"You're just the right size."
   Pip smiled a big puffed-up
pie smile. But all he said was . . .

"BURP!"

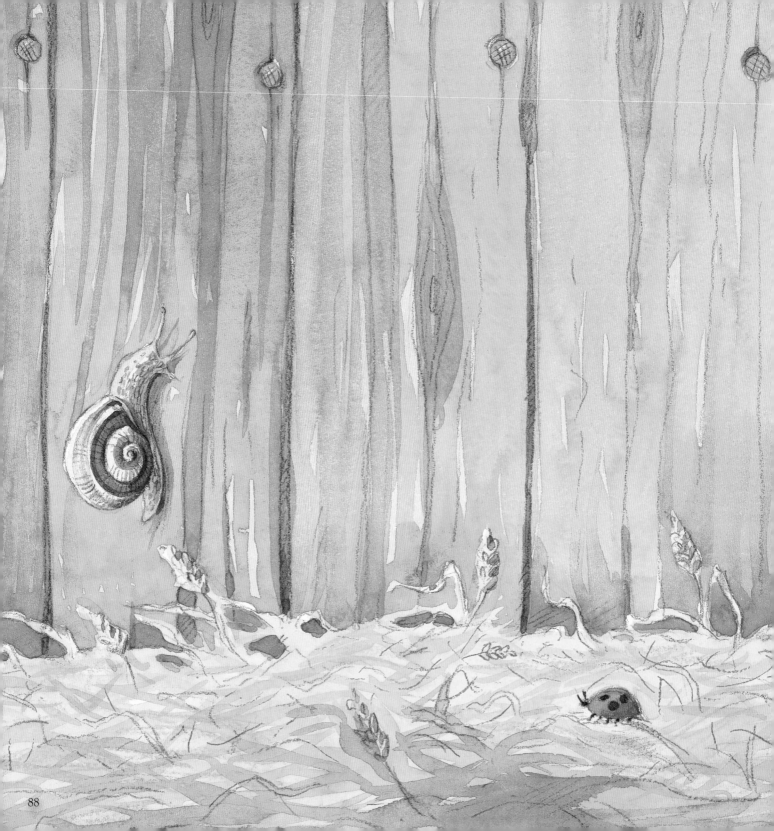

Goose
on the
Loose

Claire Freedman

Vanessa Cabban

The sun was up and shining. Red and gold autumn leaves tumbled from the trees.

"Wakey wakey, little Gooseberry!" called Mama Goose. "It's lovely weather for you to practise your flying again."

"Yippee!" Gooseberry replied.

So, after breakfast, Gooseberry flip-flapped through
the fallen leaves, all the way down to the lake.
His friend Beaver was at work in the water.

"Hey, Beaver," called Gooseberry. "Would you
like to watch me practise my take-off and landing?"

Gooseberry ran as fast as he could.

"Clear the runway! Goose on the loose!"
he shouted. "Vroom!"

He soared right over Beaver's head
and landed again with a bump!

"See that?" cried Gooseberry. "I'm getting
better and better all the time!"

"Great landing!" agreed Beaver. "But I can't
stop, Gooseberry. I must finish building my
dam before winter comes." And with a quick
wave, Beaver disappeared beneath the ripples.

Gooseberry zig-zagged through the air,
backwards and forwards across the lake.
Orange and yellow leaves tumbled from the trees.
 "I bet I could dance in the breeze like the leaves,"
said Gooseberry. He decided to try.

"Up, up and away I go!" Gooseberry cried.
It wasn't so easy. But someone was clapping!

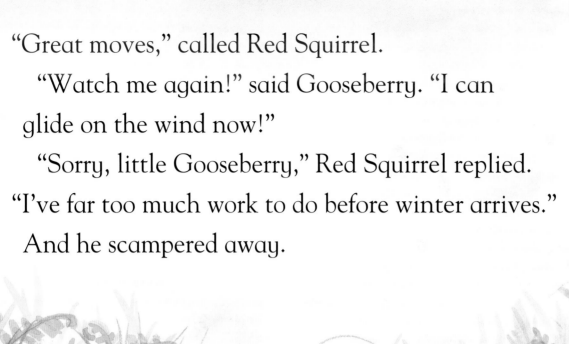

"Great moves," called Red Squirrel.

"Watch me again!" said Gooseberry. "I can glide on the wind now!"

"Sorry, little Gooseberry," Red Squirrel replied. "I've far too much work to do before winter arrives."

And he scampered away.

As Gooseberry practised his swoops
and dives he spotted his friend Mouse.
"Look at my loop the loops, Mouse!"
he called. "I can do them at last!"

"That's clever!" said Mouse. "I've no time to stop though. I'm in a hurry to build my nest."

"Yes, I know!" sighed Gooseberry. "Winter's coming!"

"You should get ready for winter too,"
Mouse called as she scurried off.
    "Maybe Mouse is right," thought Gooseberry.
    He started searching for berries
and seeds, but it was hard work. "Phew!
I'd rather practise flying!" he decided.

"I wonder how high I can fly?" thought
Gooseberry. Up, up, up the little goose
soared, and down, down, down he spiralled.
"Wheeee!" cried Gooseberry. "I couldn't do
that before!"

   "That looked scary!" called Hare from the
muddy bank.

"Did you see how high I went?" Gooseberry laughed. "I can show you again, if you like!"

"Well, I'm hard at work tidying my burrow," Hare replied. "I must get it spick and span and cosy before the snowy winter comes!" And Hare hopped down his hole in a hurry.

Suddenly a chilly breeze ruffled
Gooseberry's feathers. Winter *was* coming!
He began to feel a teeny bit worried.
Everyone was preparing for it – except him.
Gooseberry decided to fly back home
at once.

"Whatever is the matter, Gooseberry?" Mama asked.

"Winter's coming!" Gooseberry cried. "And I'm not ready!"

"Don't you remember me telling you?" Mama Goose laughed. "Geese don't stay here for winter. Brrr no!"

"We'll be flying south, to where it's lovely and warm!" Papa Goose added. "It's a long journey, and that's why you needed to practise your flying. You *have* been getting ready for winter all along!"

"So I have!" said Gooseberry happily. "I bet I could fly for miles and miles. Just watch!" And little Gooseberry dipped and dived and danced in the fading blue sky. Just like the red and gold leaves that tumbled from the trees.

The Great Goat Chase

Tony Bonning

Sally Hobson

Mr Farmer had a field
and in this field he decided
to grow turnips.
So he ploughed the field and
sowed the seeds in long neat rows,
up and down, up and down,
until the whole field was done.

120

The seeds grew and grew
and soon every row was
filled with large, round,
plump turnips.

121

Now Mr Farmer had three goats
which he milked every morning.
But one day Mr Farmer left the gate open . . .

. . . and the goats slipped through it, right into the turnip field. Straight away, they began to chomp the turnips, row after row after row.

Mr Farmer looked out of his kitchen window and saw those goats gobbling up his turnips. "Oh no!" he cried, running out of the door.

Mr Farmer tried to chase the goats out of the field.
But those goats had minds of their own. One ran this way,
one ran that way and the third ran another.

Could Mr Farmer get those goats out of the turnip field?

No, he couldn't!

"I know," said Mr Farmer. "I'll get Dog."

He gave a loud whistle and Dog came running.

He rushed into the field and tried to herd the goats.

But Dog was a *sheep*dog and these were goats!

One went this way, one went that way and the third

went another, round and round the field until . . .

. . . Dog was exhausted.

Could Dog get those goats out of the turnip field?

No, he couldn't!

As Mr Farmer and Dog were wondering what to do, Horse stuck his head over the fence. "I've got good long legs," said Horse. "I'll help you!"

Horse jumped the fence and raced up the field, sending turnips flying. Horse was bigger and faster than the goats, but they could turn more easily. One turned this way, one turned that way and the third turned another.

Could Horse get those
goats out of the turnip field?
No, he couldn't!

As Horse sat down beside Mr Farmer and Dog,
Cow came up to them.

"Let me show you how it's done," she said.

"My big horns will soon send them on their way."

And so they did.

One goat went scampering this way

one goat went scampering that way

and the third went scampering

another – every way but the right way.

Could Cow get those goats

out of the turnip field?

No, she couldn't!

Now Pig decided to show them how it was done.
"It's time to get tough," he said,
and charged with all his might . . .

One goat nimbly tripped this
way, one goat nimbly tripped that way and
the third nimbly tripped another.
Could Pig frighten the goats out of
the turnip field?

No, he couldn't!

Mr Farmer, Dog, Horse, Cow, and Pig all sat
down and cried their eyes out.

"Boohoo, boohoo, boohoo," they howled.

Just then, Little Busy Bee
came buzzing by.

"I'll get those goats out of
the turnip field," she said.

"You?" everyone exclaimed.
"A teeny weeny, tiny winy,
wee, wee bee?"

"Yes me!" she said.

137

Mr Farmer, Dog, Horse, Cow and Pig all stopped crying and began laughing and laughing instead.

When they had finished, Little Busy Bee said, "Can I go and get the goats out of the turnip field now?"

"All right, off you go!" they said, drying their eyes.

Little Busy Bee flew into the turnip field.
She buzzed round and round the goats'
heads, and then she said . . .

"IF YOU
DON'T LEAVE
THIS FIELD RIGHT NOW,
I'LL STING YOUR BOTTOMS!"

Could Little Busy Bee
get those goats out
of the turnip field?

141

YES, SHE COULD!

The goats ran as fast as their little
hooves could carry them out of
the gate, up the road and back
on to the hillside.

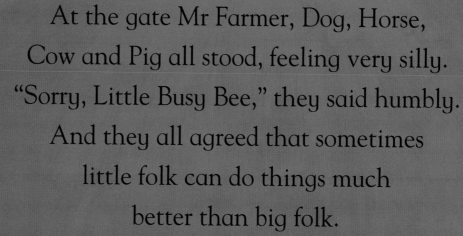

At the gate Mr Farmer, Dog, Horse,
Cow and Pig all stood, feeling very silly.
"Sorry, Little Busy Bee," they said humbly.
And they all agreed that sometimes
little folk can do things much
better than big folk.

145

Come On, Baby Duck!

Nick Ward

It was a BIG day for Baby Duck.

A VERY big day!

He was going for his first swim
and he was very excited.

"I can't wait," Baby Duck
said to Teddy. "It's going to
be brilliant. The best day ever!"

"Wait for me!" puffed Baby Duck,
waddling to catch up with
his family.

"Hurry up, slow coach," quacked
his sisters, Minnie and Molly.

"I'm going as fast as I can.
I'm only little!"

"We're nearly there, darling,"
called Mummy Duck.

Splash!

"Look at us," quacked Minnie and Molly.

"Come on, Baby Duck!" said Mummy Duck.

"It's your turn."

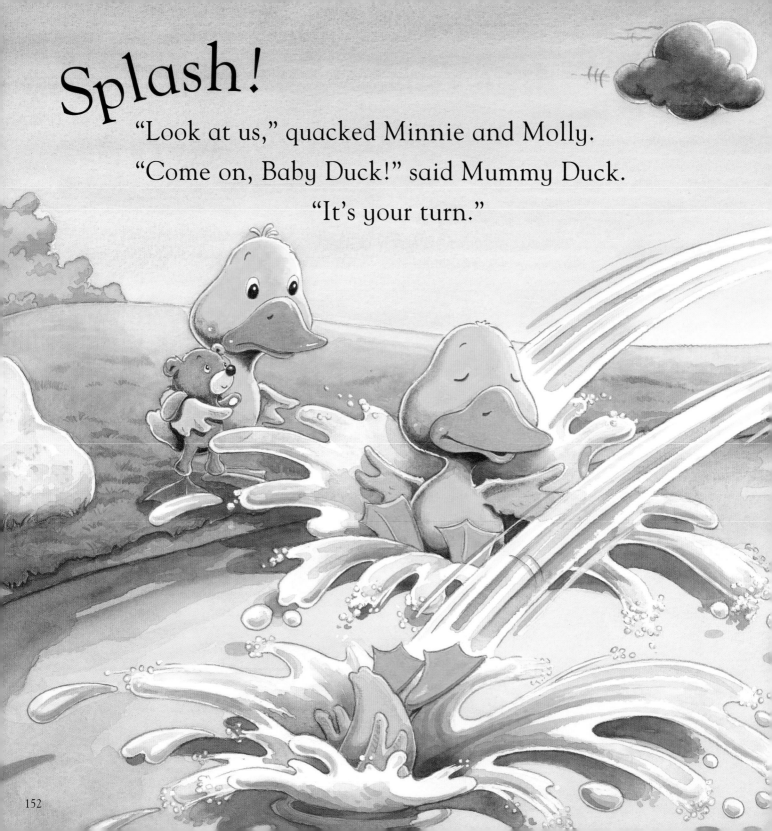

Baby Duck stood at the edge of the pond.
"It's very big," he said. "I might get lost."
"I'll stay close," said Mummy Duck.

153

Baby Duck looked into the water.

"It looks deep," he said.

"Jump! I'll catch you," smiled his mummy.

Raindrops started to plop
into the water.
Baby Duck hugged
his teddy.

Splash!

"Jump in, Baby Duck," croaked
Little Green Frog. "It's fun!"
Baby Duck dipped his toe into the water.
"It's cold!" he shivered.

"It's too deep, it's too cold and . . ."

"... it's scary!"

"My little Baby Duck!" said Mummy.
"There's nothing to be afraid of."
She gave him a great big hug.
"Let's just watch the fun for a bit."
The rain pattered down and the
wind started to blow.

Splash!

"Dive in," piped the little fish,
leaping out of the pond.
"You can do it!"

"I can't," whimpered Baby Duck,
as the wind blew harder.
"It's splashy and horrible!
I hate it!"

But just then,

whoo!

The wind blew Baby Duck's
teddy up into the air and . . .

Splash!

"Help!" cried
Baby Duck.
"Teddy can't swim!"

But everyone was too far away. "Hold on,
Teddy," called Baby Duck. "Here I come!"

Baby Duck jumped.
He dived right in
and he swam
and he swam
and he swam.

"I'm coming, Teddy,
don't worry…"

"You're safe now, Teddy!" said Baby Duck. "Well done! You did it!" cried his mummy. "You can swim!" The sun popped out from behind the clouds. Baby Duck smiled.

"I wasn't scared," said Baby Duck,
hugging his teddy. "I love the water . . .
and so does Teddy!

This is the best day ever!"

Splash!

174

This and That

Julie Sykes

Tanya Linch

Down on the farm
Cat woke early.
It was a special day and
she had work to do.

177

Horse was grazing in the field
when Cat jumped onto the fence.

"Hello, Horse," said Cat. "May I borrow your stable?"

Horse didn't use his stable in the summer because he liked to sleep outside. "Yes," he neighed. "What will you use it for?"

"This and that," purred Cat.

179

Pig was rolling in his sty
when Cat leaped onto the wall.

"Hello, Pig," said Cat. "May I have some of your straw?"

"Help yourself," grunted Pig. "There's plenty of it. But what's it for?"

"This and that," purred Cat.

Goat was playing in the yard
when Cat hopped on the gate and miaowed.

"Hello, Goat," said Cat. "May I have some hay?"
Goat never ate hay in the summer when the
grass was green and lush.

"If you want," he cried.

"Whatever do you need it for?"

"This and that," purred Cat.

Sheep was dozing under
a leafy tree when Cat
climbed onto a branch.

"Hello, Sheep," said Cat. "May I have some of your soft wool?"

Sheep had a thick white coat and plenty to spare.

"Of course you may," she bleated. "What are you going to do with it?"

"This and that," purred Cat.

Hen was scratching for grain
when Cat leaped on top of the hen house.

"Hello, Hen," said Cat. "May I have a few of your feathers?"

Hen stopped scratching and cocked her head curiously.

"You may," she clucked. "But whatever for?"

"This and that," purred Cat.

Cow was drinking from the stream
when Cat joined her on the bank.

"Hello, Cow," said Cat. "May I have a few hairs from your tail?"

"Yes," she mooed. "What are you going to do with them?"

"This and that," purred Cat.

Donkey was looking for thistles
when Cat jumped on his back.

"Hello, Donkey," said Cat. "May I borrow that lovely purple ribbon from your hat?"

"If you're careful with it," he said. "What do you want it for?"

"This and that," purred Cat.

The animals thought Cat was behaving strangely.

   "What does she want with all our things?" clucked Hen.

   "Perhaps she's moving house," mooed Cow.

   "No," grunted Pig. "Cats don't like moving."

   "Let's follow her," brayed Donkey.

So when Cat
appeared, they
tiptoed after her.

Cat went inside the stable
and the animals followed silently behind.

In one corner they saw . . .

. . . two little kittens.

They were inside a nest made from hay
and straw. It was lined with Sheep's wool,
hair from Cow's tail and feathers from Hen.
It was decorated with Donkey's pretty,
purple ribbon.

"So that's what you needed our things for!" exclaimed Sheep.

"What are they called?" asked Donkey.

Cat sighed. "I can't decide. What do you think?"

The animals looked at each other and cried

"WE KNOW . . ."

Don't Be Afraid, Little Foal

Caroline Pitcher   Jane Chapman

One moonlit night, while the wind
raged and the rain drummed on the
stable roof, a mare gave birth to her
foal. She breathed on him softly, until
he struggled up on a tangle of long legs.

"What's that noise?" asked the foal.

"Just the wind," said his mother. "When you are big you will run with the wind over the hills."

"Will you be there with me?" asked the foal.

"No," said his mother. "But you won't think of *me* at all."

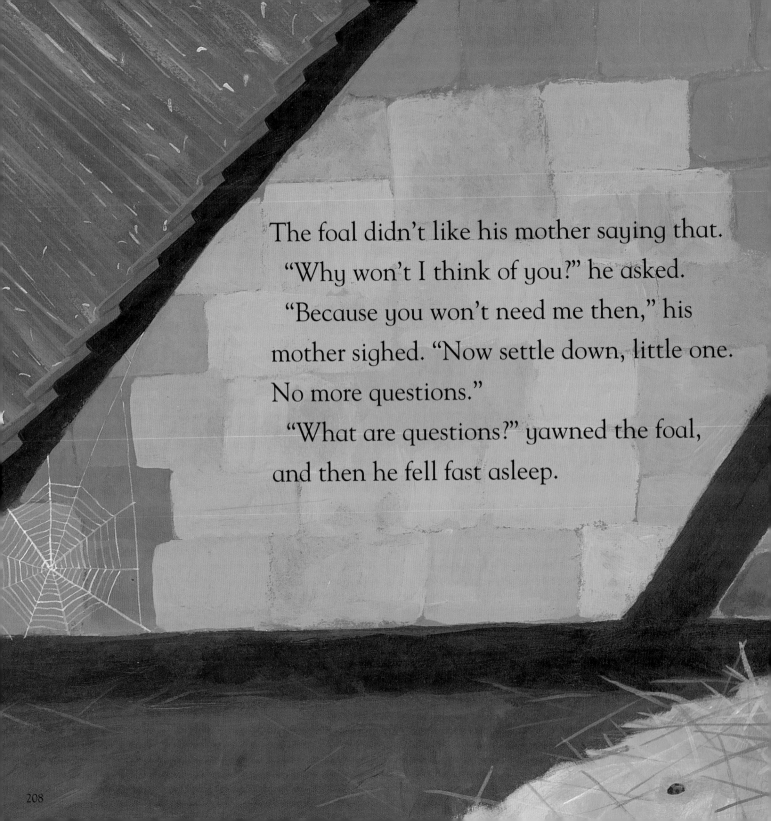

The foal didn't like his mother saying that.

"Why won't I think of you?" he asked.

"Because you won't need me then," his mother sighed. "Now settle down, little one. No more questions."

"What are questions?" yawned the foal, and then he fell fast asleep.

Spring came, and the foal's legs
grew longer and stronger, so that
his head just reached the top of
the stable door.

"What's outside?" he asked.

"It's a field," said the mare. "Soon
you will be able to go there with
me and run all the way round
and back again."

"I don't think I want to," said
the foal, drawing back. "I don't
like Outside. I like it here."

The foal's legs grew even stronger and longer. Now he could see right over the stable door. He saw a horse as dark as the night sky, and a pony as pale as moonlight. "Where are their mothers?" he asked. "They are at other stables," said the mare. "They give people rides. I'll do that again soon, too, little one, while you stay behind."

"No," said the foal, turning his back.
"I don't want to think about it."

When the days grew warmer,
the mare and her foal went out
into the field. They ran all the
way around it and back again.

Twilight fell, and the foal looked uneasy.

"Can't we go back to the stable now?" he asked.

"No," said his mother. "When the nights are warm, we stay outside."

"But it's *dark!*"

"It's dark in the stable, too, little one. But you know I'm here, even if you can't see me," whispered the mare.

The foal lifted his head out of the darkness.

"What's making that noise?" he asked.

"Just the wind," said his mother.

"But where is it?" asked the foal.

"You know it's there, but you can't see it."

"Just like you in the dark, Mum,"

he whispered.

One morning, the foal woke late.
His mother was by the fence. She
had a bridle over her head and a
saddle on her back.

"I'm going to give rides again,"
she called to him.

"And who will ride me?" cried
the foal with excitement.

"You're too little to be ridden
yet," explained his mother.

"But I'll be all alone,"
he wailed. "Oh, please stay
with me!"

"No," said the mare, as a little girl climbed onto her back. "You'll be all right. You won't think of me at all."

The foal watched as his mother and her rider trotted out of sight. He was all alone.

"Come back, Mum!" he neighed, and his voice echoed in the hills.

He heard something answer him, but it wasn't his mother. It was the wind! The wind had come down from the hills to play with him. It blew a butterfly so that the foal could chase it, and it blew a path through the meadow so that he could run right through the middle.

The foal jumped and ran and bucked and chased and flicked his little black tail. He played with the wind all morning.

And then, just as the foal was too tired to run and jump anymore, his mother came back! *Goodness*, thought the foal. *I didn't think of Mum at all – not once.*

"The wind played with me," he said.

"So you didn't think of me at all?" asked his mum.

"Maybe a *little* bit," said the foal.

"That's as it should be," said the mare. And she nuzzled her little one's neck, and gave him a kiss on the nose.

Martin Hall

Charlie and Tess

Catherine Walters

It was spring, and lambing time high up in the dark mountains. The weather was still cold and a blizzard was raging, so the farmer was out, tending his flock.

The farmer stopped and listened. What was that? A little plaintive, bleating cry.

It was a tiny lamb, alone and hungry.

"My, you're a small one," he said. "Can't find your mother, eh? Never mind, you come home with me."

In the farm kitchen the farmer's little daughter, Emily, made the lamb a cosy nest from a cardboard box and some old jumpers. He was very weak, but was soon hungrily sucking warm milk from a bottle with a teat on it.

"Let's call him Charlie," said Emily. Then, because they could find no ewe to look after him, Charlie became the family's own special pet, and lived with them in the farmhouse.

The farmer had a sheepdog called Tess, and as soon as Charlie was able to skip and frisk around in the farmyard, Tess was there to look after him.

All the time Charlie grew quickly. He was soon too big for the kitchen, so he slept outside in Tess's kennel. It was a tight squeeze, but the sheepdog and the lamb didn't mind. For they were friends, and kept each other warm.

They played together, when Tess was not working. The farmer would throw a ball and watch them both chase it. Charlie was slower than Tess, of course, but often she would let him win.

"Sometimes I wonder if Charlie's turning into a dog," the farmer's wife said, as the family watched him one day.

Charlie even had his own
collar and lead. When the
farmer's wife took Emily
down to the village with
Tess, Charlie would go
as well. The people in the
shops would laugh and
point, as Charlie walked
proudly along the road,
carrying a newspaper in
his mouth.

All too soon Charlie grew too big for the kennel. It was time for him to join the other sheep.

Up on the mountainside Charlie missed his adopted family. Tess was lonely as well without her friend, and cried by her kennel.

"Never mind, old girl," soothed the farmer. "We'll see Charlie soon enough when we have to move the flock to the next pasture."

That was when the trouble started. When the
farmer and Tess came to move the sheep to
a new field, Charlie wanted to help.

 "Charlie! Go back to the other sheep," laughed
the farmer.

   But Charlie was determined to round
up the sheep with Tess, and the farmer had to
push him back to the flock again.

Summer turned to autumn, and then it was
nearly winter again. Charlie sniffed the air.
It reminded him of a time long ago, when
he was lost and alone and cold. The sky
filled with clouds the colour of slate.

It grew colder and colder as the wind blew.
The sheep huddled together, but there was
little shelter. Then it began to snow.

Charlie baaed anxiously. Light snow began to settle on his fleece. Where was Tess? Where was the farmer? If they didn't come soon, the snow would bury the whole flock.

The snow blew into the sheep's eyes and stung them with cold. Charlie knew that they must all move down into the valley, before it was too late.

Charlie ran ahead of the flock, but they stood stock-still, for they thought only a sheepdog could round them up. Luckily Charlie knew exactly what to do. He baaed loudly. He ran back and butted them, and pulled their fleeces with his teeth. He raced backwards and forwards, until the flock began to move, all the way down the mountainside to shelter.

Many hours later the storm died down, and a low sun shone orange across the snow-covered hills.

The farmer was at last able to go out and search for his flock. He paused for a moment, looking up at the mountain.

"I'm really worried – I don't know if we will be able to find them up there," he said to Tess. Tess ran on ahead, and then she started barking.

"What have you found, girl?" he asked.

At the end of the path the farmer stood, amazed. All of the flock was safely gathered there, at the bottom of the mountains, in a sheltered hollow.

"This must have been you, Charlie," he said. "You really are a sheepdog after all!"

"Six." Baa Snore!

But counting sheep made Sam so sleepy
that he just couldn't stay awake to remember
to shut the gate. So the sheep wandered out.

One sheep got into Mrs Battersby's garden at Number Twenty-three and began eating the grass on her lawn.

One began nibbling at the clothes on
Mrs Battersby's washing line.

Mrs Battersby wasn't very happy.
She shooed away the sheep and
shouted at the farmer.

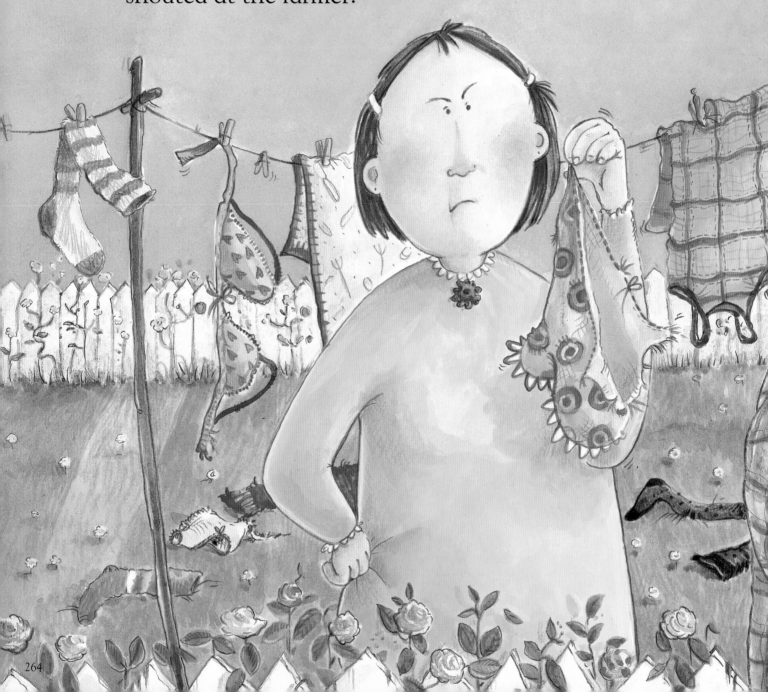

The farmer spoke to Sam. "You're a good shepherd, Sam, but you must remember to shut the gate."

The next morning, Sam got
ready to count the sheep again.
"One," he counted. Baa.

"Two." Baa.

"Three." Baa Yawn.

"Four." Baa Stretch.

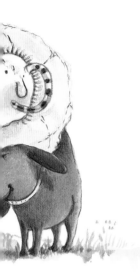

"Five." Baa Yawn.

"Six." Baa Snore!

So the sheep wandered out.

The sheep strayed into Mr Ecclestone's garden
at Number Twenty-five. They went right through
his vegetable patch . . .

And trampled all over his runner beans, and his cabbages, and his sweet peas, and his very large marrow (which he hoped would win a prize).

Mr Ecclestone was even more cross than
Mrs Battersby. He shooed away the sheep
and shouted at the farmer.

The farmer spoke to Sam. "You're a
good shepherd, Sam, but you must
remember to shut the gate."

The following day, Sam got ready to count the sheep as they came into the field.

"One," he counted. Baa.   "Two." Baa.   "Three." Baa Yawn.

So the sheep wandered out.

"Four." Baa Stretch.   "Five." Baa Yawn.   "Six." Baa Snore.

They clambered over the
hedge into Miss Flint's garden
at Number Twenty-seven.

The sheep drank from the bird-bath, kicked Miss Flint's gnomes and messed about in her pond.

Miss Flint was extremely angry. She shooed away the sheep and shouted at the farmer.

The farmer spoke to Sam. "You're not a good shepherd after all, Sam," he said. "You'll have to go."

277

The next day, Sam got a new job.

He went to work in the zoo.

He worked hard
all day long.
He fed the tigers –
a scary job.

He bathed
the hippos –
a soggy job.

He cleaned out
the elephant house
– a smelly job.

That evening, Sam stood
by the lion cage ready
to count the lions before
they went inside to sleep.

"One," he counted. Roar.
"Two." Roar.
"Three." Roar Yawn.
"Four." Roar Stretch.
"Five." Roar Yawn.
"Six." Roar Snore!

Oh yes, counting lions
made Sam sleepy too . . .

Oh dear!

5 MINUTE FARM TALES

LITTLE TIGER PRESS
1 The Coda Centre,
189 Munster Road,
London SW6 6AW
www.littletigerpress.com

First published in Great Britain 2013

Printed in China • LTP/1800/0523/1112

ISBN 978-1-84895-634-6

2 4 6 8 10 9 7 5 3 1